SP BR CAMARENA
Camarena, Cathy, 1966-
Cindi y César /

Cindi y César

Cathy Camarena, M.Ed., and Gloria B. Ruff, M.Ed.

Consulting Editors
Lourdes Flores-Hanson, M.S.E., and Gloria Rosso-White

Published by ABDO Publishing Company, 4940 Viking Drive, Edina, Minnesota 55435.

Copyright © 2006 by Abdo Consulting Group, Inc. International copyrights reserved in all countries. No part of this book may be reproduced in any form without written permission from the publisher. SandCastle™ is a trademark and logo of ABDO Publishing Company.

Printed in the United States.

Credits
Curriculum Coordinator: Nancy Tuminelly
Cover and Interior Design and Production: Mighty Media
Child Photography: Steven Wewerka, Wewerka Photography
Photo Credits: AbleStock, Photodisc

Library of Congress Cataloging-in-Publication Data

Camarena, Cathy, 1966-
　　Cindi y Cesar / Cathy Camarena, Gloria B. Ruff.
　　　　p. cm. -- (Primeros sonidos)
　　ISBN 1-59679-851-3 (hardcover)
　　ISBN 1-59679-852-1 (paperback)
　　1. Spanish language--Consonants--Juvenile literature. I. Ruff, Gloria B., 1971- II. Title. III. Series.

PC4159.C345 2006
468.2'421--dc22

　　　　　　　　　　　　　　　　　　　　　　　　　　　　　　　2005054115

SandCastle™ books are created by a professional team of educators, reading specialists, and content developers around five essential components that include phonemic awareness, phonics, vocabulary, text comprehension, and fluency. All books are written, reviewed, and leveled for guided and early intervention reading, and designed for use in shared, guided, and independent reading and writing activities to support a balanced approach to literacy instruction.

Let Us Know

After reading the book, SandCastle would like you to tell us your stories about reading. What is your favorite page? Was there something hard that you needed help with? Share the ups and downs of learning to read. We want to hear from you! To get posted on the ABDO Publishing Company Web site, send us e-mail at:

sandcastle@abdopub.com

SandCastle Level: Beginning

Cc

**ABCChDEFGH
IJKLLLMNÑOP
QRSTUVWXYZ**

**abcchdefgh
ijklllmnñop
qrstuvwxyz**

cereal

centavo

cereza

címbalos

Un ◯ es redondo.

El es bueno.

Esto es un .

La es roja.

Mira los .

Cindi mira la cereza.

La cereza es roja.

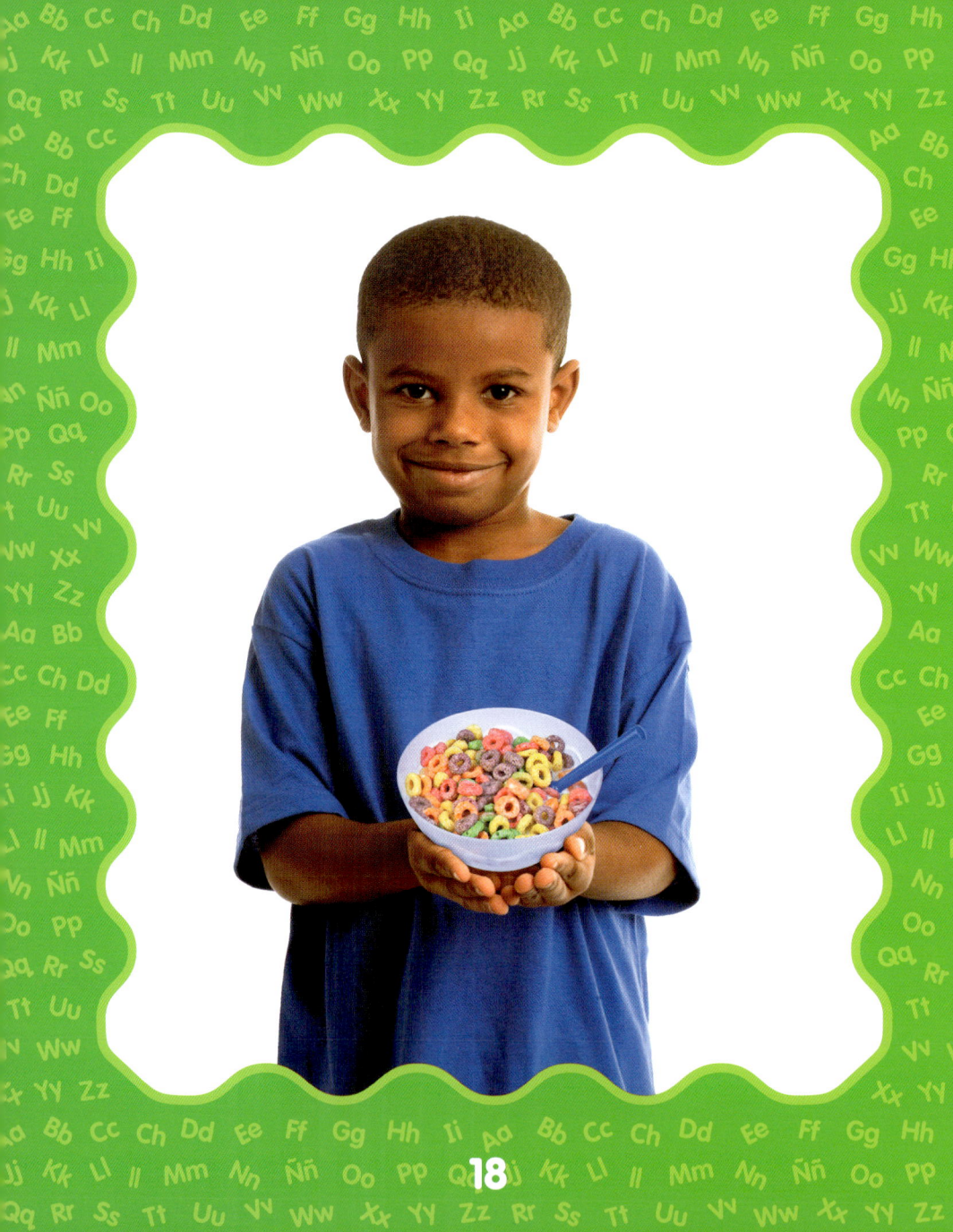

César tiene cereal.
El cereal está en un tazón.

Cindi ve cerezas en un círculo.

César ve cereal en un círculo.

¿Cuáles de estas cosas comienzan con c?

Más palabras que comienzan con c

cebolla

cebra

cepillo

cerdo

cinco

About SandCastle™

A professional team of educators, reading specialists, and content developers created the SandCastle™ series to support young readers as they develop reading skills and strategies and increase their general knowledge. The SandCastle™ series has four levels that correspond to early literacy development in young children. The levels are provided to help teachers and parents select the appropriate books for young readers.

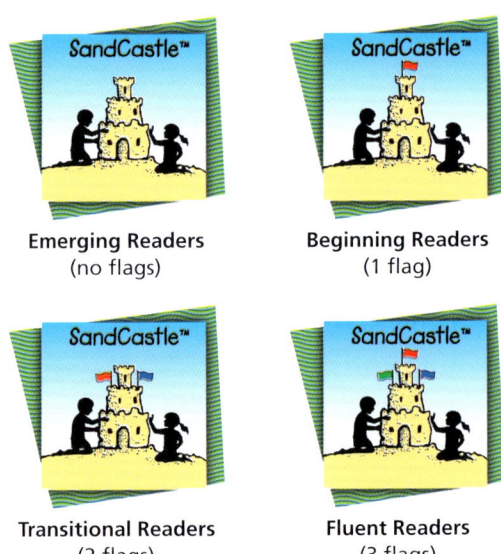

Emerging Readers
(no flags)

Beginning Readers
(1 flag)

Transitional Readers
(2 flags)

Fluent Readers
(3 flags)

These levels are meant only as a guide. All levels are subject to change.

To see a complete list of SandCastle™ books and other nonfiction titles from ABDO Publishing Company, visit **www.abdopub.com** or contact us at:
4940 Viking Drive, Edina, Minnesota 55435 • 1-800-800-1312 • fax: 1-952-831-1632